Snow White
and the
Seven Dwarfs

For Natalie - *MM*
For Kitty - *PN*

Series reading consultant: Prue Goodwin,
Reading and Language Information Centre,
University of Reading

ORCHARD BOOKS
338 Euston Road, London NW1 3BH
Orchard Books Australia
Level 17/207 Kent Street, Sydney, NSW 2000

This text was first published in Great Britain in the form
of a gift collection called *First Fairy Tales*,
illustrated by Selina Young, in 1994
First published in Great Britain in hardback in 2002
First paperback publication in 2003
This edition published in 2007 for Index Books Limited

Text © Margaret Mayo 2002
Illustrations © Philip Norman 2002

The rights of Margaret Mayo to be identified as the author and
Philip Norman to be identified as the illustrator have been
asserted by them in accordance with the Copyright, Designs and Patents Act, 1988.

A CIP catalogue record for this book is available from the British Library

ISBN 978 1 84121 154 1

1 3 5 7 9 10 8 6 4 2

Printed in China

Orchard Books is a division of Hachette Children's Books
www.orchardbooks.co.uk

FIRST FAIRY TALES

Snow White and the Seven Dwarfs

Margaret Mayo ★ Philip Norman

ORCHARD BOOKS

Once upon a time, there was a princess. Her name was Snow White and she was very pretty.

She had shiny black hair, lips as red as cherries and skin as white as snow.

When Snow White was small, her mother died and her father, the king, married again. Snow White's stepmother, the queen, was very beautiful. But she was proud and vain.

She had a magic mirror, and
when she looked in it, she said:

"Mirror, mirror on the wall,
Who is the loveliest one of all?"

And the mirror always answered:
"You are the loveliest, O Queen!"

But Snow White was growing prettier and prettier. One day, when the queen looked in the mirror, it said:

"O Queen, you are lovely, it is true,
But Snow White is far lovelier
than you!"

"Then she must die!" said the queen. She ordered a huntsman to take Snow White into the forest and kill her.

But the huntsman did not want to hurt Snow White, so he took her into the forest and left her there.

Poor Snow White walked on until she came to a cottage. She knocked at the door. When no one answered, she turned the handle and walked in.

Inside, a table was laid with seven little knives and forks, seven little loaves on seven little plates, and seven little glasses of wine.

Around the table were seven little chairs and along one wall were seven little beds.

Snow White was tired and
hungry, so she ate some bread
and drank some wine. Then, she
lay down on a bed and fell asleep.

When it was almost dark, the door opened and in came seven dwarfs. They saw Snow White and said, "Oh! What a lovely girl!"

When Snow White saw the seven dwarfs, she was surprised. But they were so friendly that she told them all about herself.

"Stay with us," they said. "But when we go to work, keep the door locked, and don't buy anything from anybody."

Every day, Snow White cleaned
the cottage and cooked, while the
seven dwarfs went to dig for gold
in the hills.

But, one day, back at the
palace, the queen looked in the
mirror and it said:

*"O Queen, you are lovely, it is true,
But Snow White is far lovelier
than you!
And in the hills, in the forest shade,
With seven dwarfs her home she
has made!"*

"She must die!" said the wicked queen. She filled a basket with ripe apples and put some poison on the rosy-red half of the biggest apple. She didn't touch the green half.

Then, she disguised herself as an old woman and off she went to the forest.

When she came to the seven dwarfs' cottage, she knocked and called, "Ripe apples for sale!"

Snow White opened the window. "I'm sorry," she said, "but I mustn't buy anything from anybody!"

The old woman picked up the biggest apple. She cut it in half and ate the green half. Then, she held out the poisoned rosy-red half and said, "Have a piece of my sweet, juicy apple!"

She seemed kind, and the apple
looked delicious, so Snow White
reached out and took it. But,
when she bit into the apple, she
fell down as if she were dead.

The wicked queen hurried back
to the palace. This time the mirror
said:

"You are the loveliest, O Queen!"

The seven dwarfs came home and found Snow White lying on the floor. They tried to wake her, but they could not.

So they made a glass coffin for
her and placed it high on a hill.

They took turns to guard it,
and for a long time Snow White
lay there, still as lovely as ever.

Then, one day, a prince came
riding by. When he saw Snow
White, he fell in love with her, and
asked the dwarfs if he could take
the glass coffin back to his father's
palace.

The dwarfs did not want to lose Snow White, but they could see that the prince loved her, so they agreed.

Then, as they lifted the coffin, one of the dwarfs stumbled and jolted it...

and the piece of poisoned apple
fell out of Snow White's mouth!
She opened her eyes and said,
"Where am I?"

How happy they all were! The
prince asked Snow White to marry
him - and she said, "Yes". Then,
she said goodbye to the seven
dwarfs and rode off with the prince.

When they reached his father's palace, everyone began to get ready for the wedding.

Now, the wicked queen was invited to the wedding. But, before she left, she looked in the mirror and asked her usual question. The mirror said:

"O Queen, you are lovely, it is true,
But the new bride is far lovelier
than you!"

"I must see this new bride!" said the queen, and she hurried off to the wedding.

When she saw that the lovely bride was Snow White, she was so full of rage that she fell down and died.

But Snow White and the prince,
and the seven dwarfs, all lived
happily ever after!

FIRST FAIRY TALES
by Margaret Mayo
Illustrated by Philip Norman

Enjoy a little more magic with these First Fairy Tales:

❏ Cinderella	1 84121 150 8	£3.99
❏ Hansel and Gretel	1 84121 148 6	£3.99
❏ Jack and the Beanstalk	1 84121 146 X	£3.99
❏ Sleeping Beauty	1 84121 144 3	£3.99
❏ Rumpelstiltskin	1 84121 152 4	£3.99
❏ Snow White	1 84121 154 0	£3.99

Colour Crackers
by Rose Impey
Illustrated by Shoo Rayner

Have you read any Colour Crackers?

❏ A Birthday for Bluebell	1 84121 228 8	£3.99
❏ Hot Dog Harris	1 84121 232 6	£3.99
❏ Tiny Tim	1 84121 240 7	£3.99
❏ Too Many Babies	1 84121 242 3	£3.99

and many other titles.

First Fairy Tales and Colour Crackers are available from all good
bookshops, or can be ordered direct from the publisher:
Orchard Books, PO BOX 29, Douglas IM99 1BQ
Credit card orders please telephone 01624 836000
or fax 01624 837033
or e-mail: bookshop@enterprise.net for details.

To order please quote title, author and ISBN
and your full name and address.
Cheques and postal orders should be
made payable to 'Bookpost plc'.
Postage and packing is FREE within the UK
(overseas customers should add £1.00 per book).

Prices and availability are subject to change.